Chance and His Backyard Buddies

RH Helm

ISBN 978-1-64569-074-0 (paperback)
ISBN 978-1-64569-860-9 (hardcover)
ISBN 978-1-64569-075-7 (digital)

Christian Faith Publishing, Inc.
832 Park Avenue
Meadville, PA 16335
www.christianfaithpublishing.com

Printed in the United States of America

Chapter 1

Home Sweet Home

Hi there, my name is Chance. I am a hummingbird. I am a really small bird, but I can fly very fast. I got my name from the man who lived in the home where I was born. I am not sure why he named me Chance, but I am sure there is some logical explanation. *What's your name?* Birds and animals don't typically have human names except for dogs and cats, but this is a different story about a special place, and it seems appropriate for all my backyard buddies to have names. The truth is most of the names came from Blue the jaybird. I will tell you about Blue later, but if you don't mind, I would like to tell you a little about myself first.

I was born at 2022 Shadow Brook Way in Henderson, Nevada. It is very important to remember your address in case you get lost and can't find your way home. That way you can tell an adult or a policeman and they can help you. Do you know your home address and phone number? Henderson is in the middle of a desert. It can be very hot and dry, but I have a beautiful home with an amazing backyard (I call it my garden). It is a great place to live. My first memory was my mother bringing me food. She would go out and catch an insect or bug and bring them back for me to eat. She also brought me nectar from flowers. I preferred the nectar because it was so sweet and delicious, but my mother said I needed to eat the insects if I wanted to grow up and be healthy. I guess it's like your mom saying you need to eat your vegetables. Moms are real smart like that. She would keep going back and forth until I was filled up. I love my mom. We lived on the front porch right above the front door of the home. The front porch provided our nest with cover from wind and rain, so we all felt very safe there. The man who lived there would come out almost every day and watch me. I don't know for sure what or why he was watching, but it sure made me feel safe. He just seemed to care how I was doing. I heard his little ones calling him Dad. It seemed to fit so that's what I decided to call him also.

Dad was there the first day I flew. I was so nervous, but Mom just kept telling me I was ready. Sometimes when you have to do something for the first time, you get nervous or a little scared, but then you find out that you can do it. So out of the nest I went. I was flapping my wings so hard I thought they might break off, but I was flying. It was awesome! I got tired pretty quickly though, so I went back to the nest, Dad seemed so pleased with me. It was a very proud moment. It is always nice to share your accomplishments with others.

I mentioned we live in a desert, but you would have never known from my house and garden. My home was an amazing place. You entered the garden through an arbor with grape vines all over it. When you past through you could pick some grapes. I don't really eat grapes, but several of my buddies do. They tell me they are sweet and delicious. Dad planted them and would watch all the birds come and eat them. He liked grapes too and would wait until they were perfectly ripe to pick them. He loved his plants as much as he loved the animals. He planted jasmine and honeysuckle so when you entered the garden, both your eyes and nose would get a real treat. It smelled so wonderful. He planted fig trees which also had a pleasant aroma when they came to life in the spring. There were apples and nectarines and lemons. There were twenty-feet-tall oleanders which surrounded the garden and made it our own private world. All the animals felt safe when living in or visiting the garden. Except when, on occasion, Cleopatra, the cat would come around and make all the little animals hide. She was always saying she just wanted to have them over for dinner, but they did not trust her intentions. Maggie the lifeguard dog would come outside, and Cleopatra would be on her way. What was I talking about? That's right, I was telling you about my garden. When you passed under the arbor, the garden started to reveal its true beauty. Dad and his two sons, Rhet and Jake, had built a big deck right above the pool. The Smiths lived under the deck. They are a mouse family, but I will have to tell you about them at another time. Past the deck was a long blue swimming pool. My buddies thought of it as more of a pond than a pool, but I knew the difference because Maggie the lifeguard dog told me. Then came a large field of grass for everyone to enjoy. The animals could hunt for insects and, early in the morning, drink the dew off of the green blades of grass. The kids could run and play all kinds of games. Sometimes the family would have a party for the whole garden. My backyard buddies loved the parties. There was music and dancing and a feast fit for a king. They would eat for weeks on what the children dropped on the ground. Yes, my garden was an amazing and wondrous place.

As I grew bigger and stronger, I began to fly all around the neighborhood. My mom would always tell me not to go too far because I might get lost, but I would get carried away and fly all over the place. I spent a lot of time flying around and exploring my neighborhood. I knew where everyone lived. I became familiar with the whole neighborhood and watched all the people as they would come and go. A lot of the big people, they were called parents, would get up early and head off for work. The little ones (they called children or kids) would stay at home and play. I especially loved watching over all the children of the neighborhood, but I liked it much better when they would come outside to play. Kids just stay inside too much these days. When the kids would come outside they would run and throw balls and some would ride bicycles. It looked like so much fun. I would hear their moms telling them to be careful and not to go too far from home (just like my mom was always telling me) but before you knew it, they would be far away from home. If you're a big kid make sure your smaller friends get home safe. We all need to watch out for each other.

One day one of the little boys (I watch over) got lost. His name is JJ. He didn't know how to get home. All the streets looked the same to him and he just couldn't remember how to get back home. He had not memorized his street address and phone number. Can you tell me your address and phone number? I could tell JJ was scared by now, but he just kept riding and riding until he got really tired. Finally he put down his bike, sat down on the curb, and started crying. It's okay to cry if you are scared. I was really worried for him because it was starting to get dark. Just as it was getting too dark to see a policewoman drove up. Police often drive through our neighborhood. Their job is to help people who are in trouble and keep them safe. They will help you, if you ever need them to. If you have a phone, you can dial 911 and the police will come and help you. The policewoman asked JJ where he lived, but he did not know. The policewoman told him not to worry she would help him get home. She asked him his name and he told her. She said, "Don't worry, JJ, everything will be fine."

She started to call on her radio when his mother and father drove up. His mom was crying so hard. It's okay to cry if you're worried or sad too. She ran up and wrapped her arms around JJ and said, "I love you, I love you. Why did you run off?"

He just held her as tight as he could and replied, "I just got lost."

JJ's father thanked the policewoman, and put JJ's bike in the back of their car and they took JJ home. I was so relieved. I can tell you, I never went too far from my home after that, because I never want to scare my mom that badly.

You should always remember your address and phone number.

Chapter 2

Maggie the Lifeguard Dog
Safety First!

I know I told you a little about my backyard or garden before, but I sure would like to tell you more. My garden was such an incredible place where animals could talk to each other and care for each other and really get along. Oh sure, we had one or two who would cause some trouble, but that is what was so special about it. All the animals would work together to overcome our problems. We were a real team when it came to looking out for each other. It is very important to work as a team. Teams can do many things someone by themselves cannot accomplish. The garden was perfect. It had decks and trees and beautiful plants. There were so many colors of flowers I could taste a new nectar every day of the month and still not get through them all. The pool was crazy big. It was the biggest pool in the neighborhood and the reason for so many of the birds first visit. They would see it from far away and drop in to enjoy it. Chuckles, the bat, flew back and forth over the pool every morning and every evening. The garden had a big grass field for the animals to find food and the children also played on it.

One of my best buddies was Maggie the lifeguard dog. She was one of the real stars of the garden. Maggie was a beautiful dog. She had short golden hair. She was such a great athlete. She loved to run and jump as high as she could. She was super fast. She loved to play sports. One of her favorite sports was soccer. Do any of you play soccer? Jake, the boy, would have his friends over to play soccer and they had such a good time. Maggie was the best soccer player of all. She would sometimes play for both teams. She would take the ball from one team and give it to the other and then turn around and do the same thing for the other team. Maggie said, "It is very important to be a good sport." She said she had heard Dad telling Jake to always be a good sport especially when you lose. Maggie was always a good sport. At the end of every game she would wait patiently until every kid got a chance to pet her. It seems she thought being a good sport was the very best part of the game.

After the kids played soccer, Hannah, Jake, and Rhet loved to go for a swim in the pool. All the kids loved the pool and sometimes there would be fifteen or twenty kids in the pool at the same time. They had so much fun splashing and playing games like Marco Polo. They would sometimes forget about safety. You see if you are going to have a pool you have to think about safety. Everyone is responsible for the safety of others. Safety rules are made to keep children from getting hurt. Maggie was a different dog when the kids went in the pool. She became Maggie the lifeguard dog. She was like a superhero. She would go back and forth the full length of the pool barking all the safety rules to the children. She would even bark at the parents if she thought they were not watching the children closely enough. The children did not understand her, but she knew all the rules. I know because she told me the most important ones.

- Don't run! You can slip and fall on concrete and really get hurt.
- Don't rough house! Smaller children can get lost in all the chaos.
- Don't go in the deep unless you are a very good swimmer and have your parents' permission.
- No diving! It is just too dangerous. So many people get hurt this way.
- Don't swim alone. Always go with a friend so you can look out for each other.
- Parents should always pay close attention. Children get excited and don't always remember the rules.
- The pool should be fenced so little ones can't get in by themselves.

Maggie was the backyard lifeguard, and she loved her work. She never took her eyes off of those kids all summer long. She would pitch a fit if the parents weren't paying attention. All her life she looked after those children. She was a good friend. The kids loved her, and she loved them even more. All those years and all those kids and no one ever got hurt. You see, Maggie told me that the best accident is the one that never happens.

Blue sang from the tree where no one could see him.
I'll make my point
Though I be curt
When Maggie's the lifeguard
No one gets hurt
For teamwork and sportsmanship
She is the best by far

But when it comes to safety

She's a real superstar.

Maggie rules! Maggie rules! Get it? Woohoo, woohoo. Then silence.

Talk about teamwork and being a good sport.

Talk about why safety is important and other things we do where safety rules should be followed—like the playground.

Chapter 3

Big Shirley and Mr. Jerome
A Chance Encounter

One sunny spring day, I was flying around in my garden having the best time when Dad showed up with Big Shirley. Big Shirley was a pigeon. She was so much bigger than me. I wasn't even sure she was a bird at first. I have come to find out there are birds much bigger than her. Big Shirley had been injured and could not fly. Dad brought her home to care for her. She told me later she flew into a car and hurt her wing. She was so scared when Dad picked her up, but later realized he was just trying to help. Dad loved helping the animals.

Big Shirley was so pretty. She had so many colors on her she looked like a rainbow. I love color. My favorite color is red. What is your favorite color? I am attracted to bright colors because that is how I find my food. I love the sweet taste of nectar I find on flowers. I have a very important job. I pollinate plants. Like bees, I am always busy from flower to flower. I love my work. I get the sweet nectar and the plants get help to. Oh, I'm sorry, I was telling you about Big Shirley. Dad didn't really have a place to put her so he made her a nest out of a large plastic bucket. He cut a doorway in the side so she could come and go and he would bring her a bowl of water and bread to eat every day. She told me she really liked the bread. "It's delicious, Chance, you should try it." It has a beautiful brown crust and a buttery flavor.

"No, thanks," I replied. "I'll just stick to my nectar. Speaking of which, I have to go. I have to keep eating all day or I won't have any energy."

"You go on, sweetie, I understand. If I ate like you, I would be as big as the car I flew into. I'll see you later."

Big Shirley was always so nice, like a grandmother. She would ask me about my mom and send her best regards. She would ask about my day and she seemed interested in every little detail, but I could tell something was bothering her. "What's a matter, Big Shirley?" I asked.

"Oh, sweetie, I am just a little lonely. I haven't seen any of my family in a long time."

It's true, she had been healing for a long time. I had not seen any of her friends or family come to visit. I know she enjoyed my visits and Dad would bring her food and say nice things to her, but I guess it is just not the same as being with your own family. I got to go home every night and see my mom, but poor Big Shirley was all alone. I didn't know what to do.

One day, I was flying flower to flower and got a little far from home. I was startled when I heard this loud flapping and cooing noise. It was coming from the rooftop of a house near to where I was enjoying some delicious roses. My curiosity got the better of me. I had to see what was making all the noise. I flew up to the rooftop, and there was the biggest pigeon I had ever seen. He was so big he looked like a truck with wings. He had a big barreled chest and muscles on his muscles, not a feather was out of place. I could tell he had been grooming himself as he was quite puffed up. Birds often spend time grooming themselves. They will even take a bath. Sure, have you ever heard of a bird bath? Then it hit me. I had an idea. I blurted out to him, "Hi, I am Chance. What's your name?" I had made so many friends by just smiling and introducing myself.

"My name is Mr. Jerome, and you can call me Mr. Jerome. I am the biggest pigeon in the whole town and the most handsome. I am so pretty all the other pigeons are jealous," he said, only slightly looking away from his reflection in the shiny metal roof. I had no reason to doubt what he said. He was big and beautiful and had a certain charm about him. He even had more color than Big Shirley, but he did seem to be a little full of himself.

"Hey, Mr. Jerome."

"Yes?"

"Do you like bread?" I asked.

"I certainly do, sir. I love bread with the golden-brown crust and the buttery flavor. Now you've done it. You've gone and made me hungry."

I had the feeling this bird was always hungry.

"Do you know where one might acquire this bread, sir?"

"I sure do, Mr. Jerome."

"Well then by all means, lead on, young bird, and show me this wondrous place. I am so tired of this dreadful dog food and bugs. It's just not fit for a gentleman."

My mom told me later pigeons will eat just about anything. They love greasy french fries even though it's not really good for them. I guess they are a little like real kids in that regard. I'm off subject again. "Follow me, Mr. Jerome, I will take you to some bread." We headed straight for home. When we got there, Dad had just brought some bread to Big Shirley and she was busy enjoying it. "Big Shirley, I brought you a friend."

Mr. Jerome was standing there in all of his glory, confident as he could be still puffy from his personal grooming.

"He don't look like much to me," she said.

What? I thought to myself. I was sure she would really like him. Mr. Jerome's feathers seemed to shrink and he lost a quarter of his size.

There was an awkward pause and then. "Mame," he said in his low voice, "you have caught me off guard. The young lad never told me such a lovely creature would be here. He only assured me there would be bread. My apologies for the intrusion. I will retire now, and again, I am sorry for any inconvenience I may have caused you."

You could tell for Mr. Jerome this was love at first sight. He was a different bird, he wasn't bragging about his muscles or how pretty he was. He was a changed bird.

This seemed to have a profound effect on Big Shirley. "Hold on now," she said. "There is plenty for two. Would you care to join me?"

The truth is Big Shirley would have eaten every bite on her own, but seemed to take to Mr. Jerome more than the bread.

"It would be both an honor and a privilege to join you, Ms. Shirley."

No one had ever called her Ms. Shirley before, but she seemed to like it and she actually changed color a little when it said it. Dad must have seen what was going on and brought out some more bread so there would be enough for the both of them. Mr. Jerome was scared out of his wits and flew up to our roof, but after Dad left, he flew right back down.

"You got all those muscles and yet you are a frighten as a little mouse," said Big Shirley and laughed in a way only Big Shirley could.

"I apologize, Ms. Shirley, I did not know his intentions."

She just laughed and said, "Well never mind. Let's eat."

They could really put away the bread. They ate and drank until every crumb was gone and then sat quietly and watched the sunset. It was a good day on Shadow Brook Way.

Don't be afraid to tell your parents or your friends if you are sad or lonely. Many times they can help cheer you up and make you feel better.

Blue appeared

If you're ever sad
maybe a little blue
please know for certain
the buddies care for you
tell your parents

or tell a friend
open your heart
and let healing come in

Blue left quietly without a hoot

Chapter 4

Ronin the Wandering Rat

I remember the first time I met Ronin. Ronin was a rat and his name suited him. He was a ship without a rudder. He just seemed to let life pass by without a worry in the world. I later found out he had come to Henderson in a railroad shipment of palm trees. He told me he was not one to put down roots because he loved to travel. He would winter in the desert and then be off to cooler climates for the summer.

It was just about dark and all my friends were settling in for the night. I was finishing up my last meal of the evening when out of the bushes, I heard someone calling out, "Hey there." I wasn't sure they were speaking to me, so I continued to drink the delicious nectar.

"Hey there, you, you little bird."

"Yes," I replied.

"You wouldn't know where a weary traveler might acquire some cheese do you? I would gladly pay for it. I have all sorts of trinkets to trade."

I had never met a rat, so I was very interested in him. He was pretty big. Way bigger than the mice that lived in the garden. He had a string wrapped three times around his waist and a large needle attached to the string. He said it was his sword and it was only to be used to protect others. He wore a headband made of a piece of red cloth with little jewels glued to it. His hair was long and dropped over the red headband except where his face was. He had a purple bag on his hip and it was loaded with all kinds of shiny objects. I was so fascinated by him I ignored his question about the cheese. I smiled and introduce myself. "Hi, my name is Chance. Welcome to my garden." My mother had told me be careful about talking to strangers, but I forgot.

"It is an honor to make your acquaintance young one. I have been on a long journey and am in need of sustenance."

To be honest I did not know what he meant, but he had asked about cheese so I thought it might have something to do with cheese. "The mouse family who lives under the deck always has cheese," I blurted out without even thinking.

"Interesting," he replied. I thought it an odd response, but continued the conversation.

"What brings you to our garden?" I asked.

"Chance, I travel the rails (speaking of the railroad). I am as free as a bird. I go where I want and I do as I wish. No one tells me how to live my life."

I wasn't convinced he really believed what he was saying, but I always try to believe the best of my buddies. The truth is, many of my bird friends leave every winter and return in the spring to have their babies. They call it migration. Oh yeah, back to the story.

The next day came early. All of the garden animals were about their daily activity when Mrs. Smith, the mouse, came running out of her nest. "The cheese is gone! The cheese is gone!" This put the garden into quite

THE SMITH FAMILY

Josephine

Nillie

Buck and Millie Smith
and the Pinkies

Billie

Sillie

Willie

a frenzy. The Smiths were a family of mice and they were very wealthy. They lived in the main house (Dad's house) in the winter months and would move out to their vacation home under the deck on the edge of the pool for the summer. It was much cooler and food was plentiful during the summer. Mice are very curious creatures and collectors of all sorts of things, so their summer home was well decorated with all kinds of human trinkets. Mice families are large and they call the babies pinkies. Maggie, the lifeguard dog, was always worried about those little pinkies getting too close to the pool and any chance she got she was barking out the rules for safety. Oh, there I go again. I am supposed to be telling you about the missing cheese.

All the backyard animals gathered around Mrs. Smith as she recited her frantic story. "It was quite lovely last night so we had dinner out by the pool. We had cheese and some bread crust that Big Shirley had given me, she such a wonderful lady. After dinner, Buck [Mrs. Smith's husband] said he would cleanup and then be off to work. I worry so much about him working the night shift, but he says it is the best time to get the things we need, so I gave him a kiss, and then I put the pinkies to bed. I always read them a bedtime story, then typically do some chores before turning in for the night. Last night I was very tired, so I went straight to bed. When I woke this morning and went into the kitchen, the cheese was gone."

"Oh my," said Big Shirley.

Mr. Jerome said in a reassuring voice, "Now don't you fret, Mrs. Smith, I am sure it will turn up somewhere." *What do you think happened to the cheese?*

I told Mrs. Smith I would fly super high and see what I could see, and off I went. As I was flying, I remembered telling Ronin about the cheese the Smiths kept at their home. I wondered if he might know what happen to it. When I got almost as high as I could fly, I saw Ronin sitting on top of the block fence which ran around the whole garden. I dove straight for him and reached him in just a few seconds. "Ronin," I cried out, "do you know anything about Mrs. Smith's missing cheese?"

"I do not," he replied.

I never thought to ask him if he even knew who Mrs. Smith was.

He went on, "I am always interested in the procurement of cheese."

He seemed to always use big words, and again I wasn't sure what he meant, just that he loved cheese and he seemed to think about it a lot.

"Let's go inquire about this missing cheese," he said. "Perhaps I might be able to make a bargain for it. Lead on, little one."

We arrived to big commotion in the garden. All the animals had gathered by now: Chuckles, the little brown bat; Cheezy and Quackers, the mallard ducks; Blue, the jay bird, and many others. Everyone had an opinion about the missing cheese. Chuckles thought it was eaten by the pinkies at night, but Mrs. Smith assured us there were no midnight snacks in her home (she did run a tight ship). Cheezy and Quackers thought it was borrowed by someone who really needed it, but Mrs. Smith was sure she would have woken up or heard something, and wouldn't they have left a note?

Blue just kept saying, "What a waste. What a waste. Perfectly good cheese, no one can taste."

Blue was a self-proclaimed poet and everything that came out of his mouth was a rhyme. I had no clue as to what had happened to the cheese, but I just wanted the mystery to be solved, so the garden could return to normal.

Then Ronin spoke up, "Mrs. Smith, I think I might be able to solve this mystery for you. I am a traveler. I go here and there as the wind (or the railroad) takes me, and I often have to barter for my food. Last night, I met this fine young bird, Chance, and inquired about trading for some cheese. He told me there was a mouse family who always had cheese so I decided to pay you a visit in hopes we might come to some arrangement."

"Did you take the cheese?" Mrs. Smith asked.

"I am Ronin," he replied as he bowed at the waist. "I would never take anything that did not belong to me and bring such dishonor on myself."

Buck showed up at this point and asked what was going on. He looked nervously at Ronin and after inquiring what all the fuss was about, he told his story. "Last night, as I was heading off to work, I happened upon Ronin. He told me he was hungry and he would like to trade for some cheese. He seemed like an honorable fellow so I agreed to make the trade. I was hoping no one would notice the missing cheese, until I had a chance to replace it. But last night while I was at work, I only found a pretzel and a small piece of chocolate. No cheese! Anyway, Ronin is a new friend and that's what happened."

Everyone was so relieved and were about to go back to their daily activity when I realized there was more to the story.

"Wait a minute, Buck!" I shouted out. "What did you get in the trade for the cheese?"

Everyone turned around and you could hear a pin drop.

"Oh yes!" Buck explained, "It was supposed to be a surprise, but I guess the cat is out of the bag."

Heads turned frantically in all directions because they thought he was talking about Cleopatra, the cat. She would come around from time to time and cause trouble for all the little animals in the garden, except for Maggie, the lifeguard dog.

"No, calm down! I meant the secret is out in the open."

"Oooh!" everyone replied with a sigh of relief.

Buck continued, "Today is Mrs. Smith's birthday, and I was really wanting to get her something special. Ronin offered me this beautiful silver bell which he pulled from his pocket and displayed to us. It was so wonderful. I thought she would really like it. She can use it to call all of us to dinner in the evening."

Mrs. Smith actually began to cry. She was so surprised and happy. "I love it, Buck, I love it! I am so sorry I spoiled the surprise."

Buck hugged her and said, "As long as you are happy, dear, so am I."

Blue started to sing:
I will tell a story
If only you say please
The day Mrs. Smith came crying
About her missing cheese
A traveler named Ronin
Said put your mind at ease.
Your Buck and I made a trade
And I think in went real well
I received a piece of cheese

And he a silver bell

Happy birthday, Mrs. Smith! Blue laughed woohoo, woohoo and flew away.

And everyone in the garden sang "Happy Birthday" to Mrs. Smith.

Chapter 5

Cheezy and Quackers
A Baker's Dozen

It was the first day of spring and like clockwork, Cheezy and Quakers came flying into the garden. They are mallard ducks and they live down by the river, but they loved to come visit and see all of the garden buddies. They also like the idea, there is plenty to eat in my garden. Dad would always pay special attention to them when they came to visit. He would bring out extra bread for them and sit by the pool and feed them. It seems everyone loves the bread but me. You would have thought it would have made the other animals jealous, but everyone loved Dad. He seemed to always know what we needed and would supply it. He does all kinds of things to help the animals. He improved Big Shirley's house, so she could see more activity in the garden. He got me a special feeder with food only hummingbirds enjoy. Mr. Jerome will eat right out of his hand now. That took some real patience on Dad's part.

Cheezy is a female duck. She is called a hen. We don't call her hen, but you will have to wait to hear that story. She lays eggs and has baby

CHEEZY and QUACKERS

PeeWee
and
Brood

ducklings. At least that is what she told us. I have never seen a duckling. She thinks it is safer for the babies to be born down by the river. She is a mom, and moms know what is best for their babies.

Quackers is a male duck. He is called a drake. It is a pretty nice name, but we all call him Quackers. He is so handsome. His head is emerald green and it shines when the sun hits it. Both he and Cheezy have beautiful blue rectangle shapes on their feathers, border by a bold black line. They really are impressive birds. They are even bigger than Mr. Jerome, but I think he is stronger. I'm sure he would think so.

Cheezy and Quakers got their names from Blue the jaybird. It is called a nickname. Quaker's real name is Drake and everyone knows it, but we all call him Quakers because Blue gave him the nickname. Do any of you have a nickname? Most of the time nicknames are fun and meant to be a term of endearment (love), but sometimes nicknames are used improperly. If you ever have someone call you a name different than yours, it may be because they really like you. If you don't like the nickname you should tell the other person so they can call you by your real name. Be very careful to respect other people's feelings when you are creating a nickname. If you know they don't like it, then please don't continue to use it. It can be very hurtful to use a nickname no one wants. Just try to imagine if you would like to be called by the same name.

Cheezy and Quakers got their nicknames from Blue, the poet, the first time they visited the garden. They had made a long flight from the river and were getting tired. Then they saw the garden from the sky. Birds used to be the only animals that could see the garden from the sky, but some people invented google earth. I heard Rhet and Jake talking about it from their window. I guess you can see everything from their computers. I wish they would spend more time out here with us, but they love those video games they play on their computer. Anyway, Drake and Hen saw the garden and the great big pool and could not resist. They went straight for the pool. They loved the water. They would bob up and down as if they were playing. I later found out this was how they feed. All of the garden buddies came out to greet them.

Big Shirley was head of the greeting committee and was the first to greet them. "Hello, my name is Big Shirley and this is Mr. Jerome."

"It is a pleasure to meet you," said Mr. Jerome.

"I'm Chance," I said, with my usual smile.

Mrs. Smith, the mouse, and all her pinkies came out as well. Buck was sleeping because he worked at night. I could hear Maggie barking from inside the house. She was very concerned about the pool safety rules being observed. Ronin the rat inquired about the possibility they may have some cheese to trade.

Drake replied, "No, we don't have any cheese, but thank you so much for the warm welcome. We are very tired because we have flown a long way. This is Hen. She is my mate. She is not feeling very well so we need a place to stay for a few days."

It was becoming quite a spectacle when Dad showed up. He must have heard Maggie barking and took a look out of the window. He brought bread and a little cheese for everyone. Drake and Hen were a little frightened at first, so they stayed in the pool, but when they saw he was feeding all the other animals they jumped right out of the pool. Dad was so impressed with those ducks. It was just like the day he brought Big Shirley home. We must have spent an hour enjoying the food and the company. Hen was the most hungry of all of us. She just kept eating. Dad even made another trip inside and brought out crackers for everyone. The crackers were a real hit. They were like the bread but crunchy. It was so much fun. As soon as Dad left, Blue showed up.

My name is Blue, he said with a grin.
I tell you a story of two ducks who flew in.
I say this with ease, because I am breezy
Hen ate the cheese, so I call her Cheezy
As far as Drake goes, a little known fact
Drake is a male and male ducks don't quack.
There was no more cheese so Drake ate the crackers
From this day forward his name shall be Quackers.
Blue laughed loudly, woohoo, woohoo and then disappeared.

Blue was always doing stuff like that. He would come and go at a moment's notice. Big Shirley was a little irritated and nervously said, "Don't pay any attention to him. He is just one crazy bird. He makes us all look silly."

Mr. Jerome said, "I must apologize for Blue. He doesn't mean any harm. He only gives you nicknames if he likes you and considers you part of the garden family."

I was about to say something when Drake said, "Those are fine nicknames. It's true. I do not quack, and Hen did enjoy the cheese. From now on, you are welcome to call us Cheezy and Quackers."

Mrs. Smith realized the time and said, "It's time for bed pinkies," and one, two, three, four, five they marched off.

Ronin finishing off a last little crumb of cheese said, "A name is a very important thing. I was given my name as well, and I have tried to live up to it. One cannot replace a bad name. One's honor is everything." Ronin was always saying stuff that was a little hard to understand, but it always seemed very thoughtful.

Cheezy said she was very tired and asked where they could stay for the next few days. Big Shirley told her, "Don't you worry 'bout a thing, little momma. There is perfect spot over in those pine trees. There is plenty of straw to make a fine nest."

Quackers walked right by her side as they headed to the pine trees. Mr. Jerome asked Big Shirley what was going on, but she just told him, "You mind your own business, Jerome, and everything will be okay." She was the only one who called him Jerome. Everyone else called him Mr. Jerome. He always did what she said so that was the end of the conversation. Everyone went their own direction for the night.

The next day awoke to Big Shirley singing with such great joy. This is such a happy day and so many things to do. I had no idea what she was talking about. Our usual day was hanging around waiting for Dad to bring the bread and water.

"Big Shirley, why are you so happy today?" I asked.

"Cheezy is expecting," she said. "I have so much to do to be prepared.

I respond, "She is expecting what?"

Big Shirley just laughed and then replied, "Why Cheezy is expecting her baby ducklings.

"When is she expecting them?" I thought maybe they were going to fly in later.

She laughed even louder this time. "No, sweetie, she is going to have her ducklings here in the garden."

This was a little confusing for me. I really didn't know how all that stuff worked so I just played along. "Oh," I said, "she is having her babies here."

"Yes," she responded and went back to her preparations. I later was able to put together the pieces of this puzzle. Ducks lay eggs in a nest and then they stay with the eggs until they hatch. That is actually how I was born, but I don't remember any of it. Ducks will usually lay between eight to twelve eggs so the whole garden waited in anticipation for the day they would hatch.

Several days went by and, I have to admit, I had completely forgotten about the ducklings. It was business as usual around the garden. I was feeding from flower to flower and having a wonderful day when I heard

Cheezy yelling. I was startled and forgot to flap my wings for a second. Then I raced over to see what was happening. As I got closer, I realized Cheezy was not yelling because she was scared or in danger. Can you can tell the difference if someone is yelling because they are scared or happy? She was yelling and crying for joy. Everyone had gathered on the outskirts of the pine trees. We were all interested in why she had so much to cry about. Then I remembered what Big Shirley said. Quackers came out first, then Cheesy followed by one, two, three, four, five, six, seven, eight; eight ducklings, it was incredible. Wait a minute, then nine, ten, eleven, and twelve followed shortly after. Everyone was so amazed twelve is such a big number of ducklings. Everybody shouted, "Hooray, hooray!"

Cheezy and Quackers have twelve ducklings, but then a silence fell over the whole garden as little duckling number thirteen came waddling out of the pine trees. The garden erupted again. Hooray for Cheezy and Quackers! Twelve is great, but thirteen is even better. A perfect baker's dozen.

Blue appear as if from nowhere to sing this song

Cheezy and Quackers came to visit one day

The place was so pleasant they decided to stay

Big Shirley suggested a nest by the trees

Cheezy was grateful her mind put at ease

Day past by day until the ducklings did hatch

The number so large there's seldom a match

I will only speak once and I will not lie

Number thirteen was a cute little guy

Remember the day that the garden was buzzin'

The day Cheezy and Quackers had a true baker's dozen

Congratulation, Cheezy and Quackers! Woohoo, woohoo and Blue was gone.

Chapter 6

Ronin, Chuckles and Cleopatra
You Won't Like Me When I'm Hungry

It was one of those special days in the garden. There was a slight cool breeze causing the flowers to sway as if they were dancing. The sun was bright and warm and it was drawing everyone out to work or play. Kids around the neighborhood were riding their bikes and playing basketball and all sorts of outdoor games. My backyard buddies were all about their daily chores. Big Shirley was cleaning out her nest. Cheezy and Quackers were taking the ducklings for a swim. There were thirteen ducklings and they all loved to swim, but the last one was still pretty small. Blue named him Peewee because he was smaller than all the other ducklings. Peewee had a difficult time getting out of the pool. So when Cheezy told her plump (that is what you call a group of young ducklings) it was time to go, Peewee struggled to keep up. Cheezy loved the little one and was very patient with him, but she wouldn't help him. She said, "You have to learn these things, Peewee, so you can take care of yourself if I am not around to help. Practice makes perfect."

Can you think of anything you do easily now that was difficult when you first tried it? Peewee was a determined little duckling and he just kept trying until he made it out of the pool.

Cheezy was so proud of him and let him know it. "You are special, Peewee, some day you will do something really important."

One of my best friends in the garden is Chuckles. Chuckles is a canyon bat. Canyon bats live in caves, under bridges or sometimes in the attics of old houses. Most people don't care for bats, but Dad loved Chuckles as much as me. Chuckles ate all the mosquitos and insects that would fly around the pool and bite us. Did you know that bats can eat half of their body weight in insects every day? All the animals enjoyed watching Chuckles do his work. He was an amazing pilot. He wore a little leather flying cap on his head, a scarf around his neck, and goggles over his eyes. He looked like an old time pilot. Sometimes before dark, the backyard buddies would gather on the deck and watch his aerial show. He was a real barnstormer. He would dive down right to the edge of the pool and scoop up the insects right off of the surface. He would change directions on a dime. He was perpetual motion. It was fun to watch him fly.

Chuckles was the best kind of friend. He was always there when you needed him. Do you have any friends like Chuckles? A good friend is better than sweet nectar. I have lots of friends, but only one best friend and that is Chuckles. He would tell me, "If you ever need me just call and I will be there in a flash."

Cleopatra is an Egyptian Mau. She is no ordinary cat. She is very attractive and you can tell she is spoiled by her people. She wears golden earrings in both ears and a beautiful scarf of rich purple color that is made of silk with a medallion hanging around her neck. She has long claws painted gold like a lady's fingernails. They looked like needles at the end as if she has been polishing and sharpening them. She says she is descended from a line of queens going all the way back to ancient Egypt. She had eight big male mice that walked beside her. Four mice on each side carrying a long wooden stick on their shoulders. The sticks had a piece of beautiful purple cloth that extended all the way around her and hung to the ground. It made it appear like she was being carried by the mice, but she was just walking between them. Those mice seemed to be under some kind of spell. She made them stop at the edge of the garden and wait for her there.

She was the only animal that Dad refused to feed. He said she should stay on her side of the fence and out of the garden altogether. Maggie, the lifeguard dog, didn't like Cleopatra at all. Maggie was the only animal in the garden Cleopatra was concerned about. She didn't come around when Maggie was outside. She has a way about her that really scares most of my backyard buddies. They all scattered when she came around with the exception of Ronin. He is the only animal in the garden (besides Maggie) that is not afraid of her. He's not afraid of anything. He told me it comes from his discipline and training. He also told me he and Cleopatra were mortal enemies. I am not sure what he meant, but I think it means they will never be friends. Anyway, he just goes about his regular business when Cleopatra comes around. My mom told me to avoid her because she was nothing but trouble, but I think she just really needs a friend. I do keep a safe distance when she visits, but I find her so interesting. You'll almost feel hypnotized when you are in her presence.

"Chance, is that dreadful dog Maggie around today?" she asked. "She vexes me so. I am so vexed by her existence."

"No," I replied. Maggie took Rhet and Jake to the park.

"Oh, what a relief," she said with a long sigh. Cleopatra immediately turned to her favorite subject—Cleopatra. She was always talking about… well, her. Cleopatra loves some Cleopatra. "Chance, fly down here beside your queen. I require your service. If the animals see you flying at my side, they will serve and obey me also."

"I will just stay up here, Cleo."

"Don't you dare call me Cleo. It is disrespectful to your queen. You will only address me as Queen Cleopatra. I don't know how I tolerate such treatment. It's just not fitting for a queen."

"Oh, I am sorry, Queen Cleopatra, to what do we owe the honor of your visit?"

"Well, the truth is I am throwing a grand dinner party. Everyone important will be there and I wanted to invite the garden animals to come join me. They're so delicious—I mean the dinner will be delicious. Would you be a dear and make sure all the animals are invited. Especially the little ones. I enjoy them so much."

"I would be happy to," I replied.

"Now I must depart for all of this conversation has tried me. So many recipes and preparations to consider." She turned and sauntered away. Her mice met her at the edge of the garden and the royal procession ensued. It was quite a site.

I was so excited I went to Big Shirley's and Mr. Jerome's home first. "Queen Cleopatra cordially invites you to a dinner party tonight."

Big Shirley said, "She ain't no queen. She is just an ordinary house cat."

Mr. Jerome asked, "What is on the menu?"

Big Shirley said, "You will be if you go."

"Oh, I see," replied Mr. Jerome. We will not be attending the dinner party, Chance, but thank you so much for bringing the invitation."

Big Shirley said, "Sweetie, you need to avoid Cleopatra or she'll have you for dinner."

THE SMITH FAMILY

Josephine

Nillie

Buck and Millie Smith
and the Pinkies

Billie

Sillie

Willie

I was a little confused, but I flew on to the Smiths' house. The Smiths were a mouse family who lived under the deck, by the pool, for the summer. Mrs. Smith had just put the pinkees down for a nap and was sitting in her little rocking chair on the deck knitting little sweaters for the pinkees.

"Hello, Mrs. Smith."

"Why, hello, Chance. Are you enjoying this beautiful day?"

"Oh yes, I am and I have an exciting news."

"Then by all means, share it," she said.

"You and your whole family are invited to Queen Cleopatra's house for a dinner party."

"Oh no, oh no, Chance," Mrs. Smith said, almost trembling. "We can't go. We won't go. That dreadful cat had Buck under here spell once before and I almost lost him. She is no friend of ours. Chance, you need to stay away from her at all cost."

Next I visited Ronin. "How are you today, Ronin?"

"I am well, young one."

"I was sent to invite you to a dinner party."

"Is Big Shirley having a dinner party? She always hosts the most elegant parties."

"No, it's Queen Cleopatra."

Ronin immediately drew the silver needle (his sword) from the strings around his waist. "Is she here now in the garden? Where is that vile creature? Today is a good day for battle. I knew this day would come, and I am prepared to face my mortal enemy."

"No, no, she went home," I responded, hoping to ease his mind.

Then Ronin spoke, "I must give you some sage advice little one. That cat is a predator. She is a great hunter from times past. She will not only have you for dinner, but the whole garden will be her prey. Avoid the enemy and avoid conflict. The best battle is the one never fought."

I really had no idea what Ronin was talking about. As I flew away I thought, *Why doesn't anyone want to go to her dinner party?* It seems real sad. Poor Queen Cleopatra will have no one for dinner.

I went home for the evening and told my mom all about my day. My mom was very upset with me and warned me to keep clear of Cleopatra. "She doesn't want to have you over for dinner. She wants you to be her dinner."

"Oh no, now I understand. She was going to have the little ones for dinner. That's just awful!"

The next morning, I was having my early meal when Cleopatra came strolling up. "Chance," she said, "no one came to my party. Did you invite all the animals as I commanded you?"

"I sure did, Queen Cleopatra, but they didn't want to go. They said you had bad intentions toward them."

"Those rebellious subjects. How dare they ignore my invitation! Don't they know who I am? Their queen demands their attendance. Okay then, if they won't come to me, you must take me to them." She headed straight for the garden.

"Queen Cleopatra, I would be happy to deliver a message for you."

"No, I am going to teach these wretches a lesson once and for all."

Big Shirley and Mr. Jerome saw her coming and flew up to the roof top.

"I insist you come down here right now," Cleopatra said.

"I insist you leave my yard," Big Shirley shouted back.

"You will pay for your disobedience," replied Cleopatra and she turned and headed for the Smiths' house.

Mrs. Smith hurried her pinkies into the safety of the deck.

"I have come for your pinkees, Mrs. Smith," Cleopatra exclaimed in a frightening voice.

Mrs. Smith just kept yelling, "Help! Help me, somebody! Please help me!"

Cleopatra was putting her whole front leg and paw in the small hole the mouse family used as a door. She was digging with her other paw to go under the doorway and reach the little pinkies who were huddle in the corner of their home crying.

Mrs. Smith had positioned herself between Cleopatra and the pinkees and was using a little broom to push back Cleopatra's paw. No one realized it but little Peewee, the duckling, had found a spot he could squeeze through and was assisting the pinkees in a harrowing escape. I started to yell for help as well because I knew it was just a matter of time before Cleopatra broke through.

She snarled at Mrs. Smith, "After I have the pinkies for dinner, I'll have you for desert."

From the bushes, Ronin appeared, his sword drawn and ready for battle. He spoke loudly for the first time. "Cleo, Cleo, I'm the one you want."

He got Cleopatra's attention and the epic battle began. I'll teach you to address your queen in such a manner," Cleopatra declared.

Ronin did not reply as he steadied himself for what was to come. He was so brave. She was four or five times his size, but he did not back down, not even an inch.

"You'll be my main course tonight," the queen snarled.

Ronin replied, "Let the one who finishes the fight be the one to boast."

Cleopatra took a big swipe with her claws fully extended. They must have been two inches long. Ronin repelled her attack by blocking her paw with his sword, but he was knocked backward. She lounged for him with both paws extended, but he was able to evade her. The battle went on and on, and I could tell Ronin was tiring. She was just too big and strong, but he held his ground.

Out of nowhere appeared Chuckles. Chuckles dove right at Cleopatra and pricked a flew hairs off of her back just like he was scooping insects off of the surface of the pool. She screeched and spun around, but by the time she turned he was gone. Again she turned her fury to Ronin. "What's the matter, Ronin? Are you getting tired?"

Ronin wiped the sweat from his brow and replied, "My will is strong, you wretched beast."

Again Chuckles made another pass barely escaping one of her claws, but distracting her just enough so Ronin could make his move. He jumped over her head in a somersault fashion. She swung as he twisted in the air avoiding her sharp claws. He stuck the landing with both of his hind feet and struck the faithful blow. His sword plunged into her tail and the scream was blood

curdling. It had its intended effect. Queen Cleopatra leaped four feet in the air and was already running before she hit the ground. She jumped the fence and was long gone.

Everyone in the garden cheered, "Hooray for Ronin! Defender of the garden! Hooray for Ronin!"

Ronin was still breathing heavily from the battle when he spoke. "I am not the hero. Peewee led the pinkies to safety, and Chuckles showed his valor. They are the true heroes of the garden."

At that, the entire garden erupted in cheers. "Hooray for Chuckles! Hooray for Peewee! Hooray for Ronin! Defenders of the garden!"

Cheezy could not get the smile off of her face. Peewee, her smallest duckling, had proved that being small does not prevent you from being great.

Yes, Blue showed up.
The queen threw a party
but nobody came.
Cleopatra was angry
with no one to blame.
She went for the pinkies
Mrs. Smith made her stand.
Armed with no more
than a broom in her hand.
She held back the cat
as long as she could.
While Peewee helped the pinkies
through a hole in the wood.

Ronin appeared
in battle array
Years of hard training
prepared for this day.
The fight was epic
in went on for a hour
Ronin dug deep
and drew on will power
Cleopatra was stronger
and pressed the fight
She could not have expected
Chuckles faithful flight.
He dove down with precision
his aerial attack
He plucked two hairs
right off the queen's back
The brave little pilot
never did rattle
The cat though distracted
continued the battle.
Chuckles was aware
this could be Ronin's end
So he dove a second time
and did it again.
Who would have thought
such a small subtraction
Would have created

the perfect distraction
Ronin's heart was pounding
Inside of his chest
One last maneuver.
it must be his best.
He leaped over Cleopatra
twisting and flipping
He stuck the landing
the sword firmly gripping.
He drove his sword
like a hammer and nail
Right in the center
of Cleopatra's tail.
Order restored
the mighty have fallin'
It will be a long time
before the queen comes a callin'
Excellent teamwork! Woohoo, woohoo, and Blue was gone.

About the Author

RH Helm was born in 1958 in Yokosuka, Japan. Graduated from AGTS with a master of arts in missiology. He spent his early years traveling with his family at the discretion of the US Navy. The opportunity to see so many amazing places helped create his vivid imagination. Spending two years on Kodiak Island, Alaska, he wrote his first book report about the Kodiak bear. This certainly sparked an interest in animals from a young age. Eventually the family settled in Georgia where he spent his teenage years. This is where he was exposed to the rich storytelling tradition of the deep south. One of his major influences is the late great Jerry Clower, a southern comedian and storyteller. A poet of forty years, Rich has incorporated poetry into his storytelling. Your child will love this book and hopefully, it will take them on a journey of and into their imagination. An imagination is a terrible thing to waste. Happy reading!

Chance and His Backyard Buddies will take your child on an expedition into their imagination. Chance, the moderator, is a hummingbird who thinks the best of everyone he meets. He loves nectar, but he loves his buddies even more. Your child will experience rich characters like Big Shirley, the rescued pigeon, who becomes the mom of all the garden animals. Ronin, the samurai warrior, a traveling rat who rescues the garden animals from Cleopatra the cat—who thinks she descended from a line of queens from ancient Egypt. A blue jay named Blue, a loony poet will introduce poetry as a means of storytelling which will delight any-age reader. The stories, while humorous and entertaining, are designed to impart life lessons to your child. Teamwork, honor, and caring for others are woven into every chapter. Give this little hummingbird a "Chance" to fill your child's heart with joy and wonder.